1 An eighteenth-century instrument-maker's workshop, from Diderot's Encyclopaedia

Your Book of Music

The *Your Book* Series

Abbeys · Acting · Aeromodelling · Anglo-Saxon England · Aquaria · Archaeology · Astronomy · Ballet · Brasses · Breadmaking · Butterflies and Moths · Camping · Canals · The Way a Car Works · Card Games · Chess · Corn Dollies · Medieval and Tudor Costume · Dinghy Sailing · Embroidery · English Country Dancing · Film-making · Fishes · Flower Arranging · Flower Making · Forestry · The Guitar · Gymnastics · Hovercraft · Industrial Archaeology · Judo · Knots · Landscape Drawing · Light · Magic · Men in Space · Mental Magic · Modelling · Music · Painting · Paper Folding · Parliament · Patchwork · Pet Keeping · Keeping Ponies · Prehistoric Animals · Prehistoric Britain · Pressed and Dried Flowers · Racing and Sports Cars · The Recorder · Sea Fishing · The Seashore · Secret Writing · Shell Collecting · Soccer · Steam Railway Preservation · Swimming · Survival Swimming and Life Saving · Table Tricks · Tall Ships · Tennis · Traction Engines · Watching Wild Life · Woodwork.

Your Book of Music

MICHAEL SHORT

faber and faber

First published in 1982
by Faber and Faber Ltd
3 Queen Square London WC1 N3 AU
Printed in Great Britain by
Fakenham Press Limited, Fakenham Norfolk

Library of Congress Cataloging in Publication Data

Short, Michael, 1937–
  Your book of music.

  Summary: A general introduction to music with dis-
cussions of instrumental, orchestral, vocal, folk, jazz,
pop, and electronic music.
    1. Music—Instruction and study—Juvenile.   [1. Music]
I. Title
MT6 .S477 Y7 1983   780   82–9377
ISBN 0–571–18031–0   AACR2

British Library Cataloguing in Publication Data

Short, Michael
  Your book of music.
  1. Music—Analysis, appreciation
  I. Title
  780.1'5   MT6

ISBN 0–571–18031–0

Contents

Foreword

A previous book on music in the *Your Book* series
was written by Imogen Holst. In preparing this
new book I have not attempted to alter or add to
Miss Holst's work, but have completely rewritten
the text and provided a new set of illustrations. I
am grateful to Miss Holst for her suggestions in
the early stages of drafting some of the chapters of
this book.

MICHAEL SHORT

Equivalent Terms

Many words in music are understood internationally, but there are some differences between English and American terms. The main ones are as follows:

English	American
Note	Tone
Bar	Measure
Semibreve	Whole-note
Minim	Half-note
Crotchet	Quarter-note
Quaver	Eighth-note
Semiquaver	Sixteenth-note
Demisemiquaver	Thirtysecond-note

CHAPTER ONE

How music began

However far you look back into history, you will find that music has always been an important part of human life. In fact, the further back in time you go, the more important music seems to have been, so that for primitive men music was not just a luxury but was as essential to everyday existence as food, warmth and clothing. Of course, we cannot travel back in time to prove this, but we can look around the world at the customs of people who live in primitive conditions, and we generally find that music is very important to them. And it always has its own definite job to do, rather than being listened to simply for its own sake.

Perhaps the first music was made when men began to use their voices to imitate the calls of animals and birds, so that they could be lured and caught. Of course, this is not really what we mean by music, but these hunters soon discovered how to make whistles out of bone or bamboo to imitate bird calls, and in this way the first musical instruments were invented. Indians in the Amazon jungles still use these small whistles on their hunting expeditions. Another simple way of making sounds is by banging sticks together, or by hitting a stone with a stick, perhaps to frighten off wild animals, or to scare birds away from planted seeds, as was done in Ancient Egypt. This simple idea opened up possibilities for the invention of rhythmic patterns, which can be very effective without the addition of any melody.

As life became more organized, people found that music was a great help in getting through the daily work that had to be done. Jobs such as sowing the seeds, harvesting or shifting heavy loads were not so boring if songs were sung while working, and particular kinds of music became associated with particular kinds of work. For centuries, sailors sang sea-shanties while carrying out jobs on board ships, while on Ancient Greek and Roman ships the slaves who rowed at the oars were kept in time by a drummer who beat out a rhythm according to the speed required. Today we have "piped" music in factories and supermarkets to help people get through boring tasks, and radio programmes to relieve the monotony of housework.

2 A pair of double pipes, as shown on an Ancient Greek vase

3 Lurs: the ceremonial horns of prehistoric Denmark

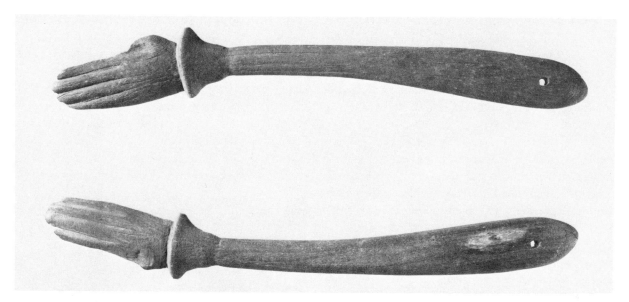

4 A pair of wooden clappers from Ancient Egypt

From the earliest times, mothers have found that the best way to get a baby to sleep is to sing some soothing music, and these lullabies are some of the most expressive songs that have ever been created.

For sounding an alarm, bells and gongs were often used, and were also used to give time signals (bells are still used as time signals on ships). Other types of signal or message can be sent by means of drums or other instruments; for example, in Nigeria the "talking drums" imitate the speech patterns of the Yoruba people, so that messages can be sent over long distances. In fairs and circuses, a roll on the drum is traditionally used to attract attention, with the shout: "Roll up, roll up!"

Music has always been widely used for military purposes: before the days of radio or the telephone, trumpets or bugles were used for sending orders over a distance, while rousing music was and is still used to help soldiers march long distances, to encourage morale, and to strike fear into the enemy.

When the day's activities were over, music could be used for relaxation, but even in this form it often served a practical purpose. The spirituals sung by Negro slaves in the American cotton plantations expressed their feelings and desire for a better life, while for people who could not read or write, stories, legends and history were passed on by word of mouth by singing them to music. The ancient Greek epic poems the *Iliad* and the *Odyssey* were probably sung to music, as this is often a great help in remembering the words. Many folksingers find that they cannot remember the words of their songs unless they sing the tune as well, and we still use little rhymes which have musical rhythms such as "Thirty days hath November . . ." or "i before e, except after c . . ." to recall information which would otherwise be difficult to remember.

People soon found that music could be used to add importance to social ceremonies; the best instruments for this are of course the louder ones, particularly trumpets and drums. In many African tribes the drums are held in great respect, because they are symbols of royalty, and in Britain today no State ceremony is complete without a fanfare from the trumpeters of the Household Cavalry to add dignity to the occasion. In Ancient China, a particular musical note was chosen to symbolize the State itself, and was regulated by the Imperial Bureau of Weights and Measures.

5 *"Talking drums" from the Ashanti region of Ghana*

As well as being used to accompany plays and other theatrical events, music is widely considered to be essential for religious worship. In the Christian church, music has been used from the earliest times, and even people who don't go to church are familiar with many hymns and carols. Many people who get married in church ask the organist to play Mendelssohn's *Wedding March*, without which the ceremony would not seem complete. In some religions dancing is closely associated with the music, while in others particular instruments are important. In India, for example, the flute is the instrument of the Hindu god Krishna, who played it to make the plants grow and the birds sing. Sometimes music is used to call upon supernatural forces: to bring rain in time of drought, or to drive away evil spirits.

Most of all, however, music is used to express human emotion, whether it be love, longing, frustration, bereavement, or simple happiness, particularly at social events such as weddings or other celebrations. Expressing emotion in music, or having someone else do it for them, makes people feel better, and makes life feel worth living.

CHAPTER TWO

How musical sounds are made

Music is a special, organized kind of sound, but it obeys the same principles as any other kind of sound. The study of the way sounds are made and behave is called Acoustics; it can tell us a lot about music and why it sounds so special to us.

Sounds are usually made when air is set in vibration; if there is a vacuum, there can be no sound (but sounds can travel through other materials as well as air, particularly water, which is how whales and dolphins communicate with each other). When we say that sound "travels through" air, this is really just a figure of speech, because the air itself doesn't travel along, but simply vibrates slightly, pushing the air in front, so that an illusion of a travelling sound wave is produced. This is rather like the effect when a railway train is being shunted; the engine pushes the first wagon, which hits the next one, and so on right down the train until the last wagon is pushed forward.

The vibrations which produce musical sounds are very fast: even the slowest ones which produce the lowest notes vibrate at least 20 times a second, while some of the highest notes vibrate 20,000 times every second! These vibrations are of course too fast to be counted, but they can be measured with special electronic equipment. The rate of vibration of a sound is called "frequency" by scientists, but musicians call it "pitch". High-pitched sounds have a fast rate of vibration, and are produced by short strings or small pipes, while low-pitched sounds vibrate less quickly and are produced by long strings or tubes.

Musical instruments can be grouped according to how these vibrations are produced. One of the most familiar groups is the stringed instruments, which, besides orchestral instruments such as the violin, viola and cello, also includes the guitar, the harp and the piano. In all these instruments the air is set into motion by vibrating strings. The pitch of the vibrations depends on the length of the string, its tension (how tight it is), its thickness, and the material it is made of. A thin, light string will produce a higher pitch than a thick, heavy one; if you look inside a piano, you will see that the lowest strings are made of much thicker wire than the higher ones. A tight string will produce a higher pitch than a string of the same thickness and material at a lower tension. All stringed instruments have arrangements for the adjustment of the tension of the strings so that different pitches can be produced. On instruments such as the violin and guitar, the player can place his fingers on each string so as to reduce its sounding length and produce higher pitches, but instruments such as the piano have a separate string for every pitch. The harp has a set of strings whose tension can be adjusted to a limited extent by means of pedals.

Although a vibrating string can make a sound by itself, its vibrations are usually too weak to move the air sufficiently to produce a loud enough sound. This is why instruments such as the violin and guitar have a wooden body: to amplify the vibrations and make the sound loud enough for people to hear. The wooden body and the air

6 A harp, with pedals for changing the pitch of the strings

inside it "resonate" when a note is played, and so make it sound louder (the body of an electric guitar, on the other hand, is only ornamental, because the vibrations are picked up electrically from the strings and passed through an electronic amplifier). Even a piano has a special wooden board behind the strings to amplify the sound.

When a string vibrates, the pitch which the listener usually hears is of the whole length vibrating:

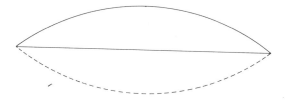

This is called the "fundamental" pitch. But the string also vibrates in halves, thirds, quarters, etc., although so faintly that they can hardly be heard. These notes are called "harmonics" or "partials":

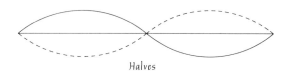

Halves

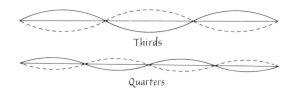

Thirds

Quarters

All these vibrations happen at the same time, and get mixed together to produce the sound you hear:

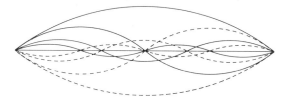

It is this mixture of harmonics which gives the individual character to the sound of each instrument, and makes the "tone" of a violin sound quite different from that of a guitar.

The whole series of harmonics produced by a string vibrating in halves, thirds, quarters, etc., is called the "harmonic series". The same effect is also produced by woodwind and brass instruments.

When a string is played with a bow, its position on the string affects the mixture of harmonics and so alters the quality of the sound which is produced. If the string is plucked, a completely different sound is produced, because of the different mixture of harmonics. Guitarists often use a small piece of plastic called a "plectrum" to pluck the strings, to obtain a more strident sound.

7 *The Spanish, or classical, guitar, in which the wooden body of the instrument amplifies the sound of the strings*

8 *The viola da gamba, showing the gut frets which guide the player's fingers on the strings*

9 *The flute is made to sound by blowing across a special hole: the formation of the player's lips is called the "embouchure"*

In wind instruments, it is the air inside the instrument which vibrates to produce the sound. All the player does is to set the air in motion. In some instruments, such as the flute and recorder, the player's breath is directed against a sharp edge, setting the air in vibration, while in instruments such as the clarinet and saxophone, the player's breath sets a reed in motion in the mouthpiece, and this in turn vibrates the air in the tube. The oboe and bassoon have double reeds, which give a completely different quality of tone from single-reed instruments, because of the different mixture of harmonics which is produced. In brass instruments, the air is set in motion by the player's lips vibrating in a cup-shaped mouthpiece.

To obtain different pitches in woodwind instruments, holes are provided which can be covered by the player's fingers or by pads, so that the length of air which is vibrating can be altered while playing. In brass instruments, the length of air is changed either by means of a slide (in the case of the trombone), or by valves (in the horn and trumpet). These devices enable extra lengths of tubing to be brought into use, and by using the lips to produce the harmonic series, a whole range of notes can be played.

The third main group of instruments is the

percussion, which consists of objects which give out a sound when they are hit. Some of them vibrate at a definite pitch, such as the bars on a xylophone or glockenspiel, while others, such as the cymbals or snare drum, give out such a complex mixture of harmonics that it is impossible to hear any definite pitch in the resulting sound.

CHAPTER THREE

The instruments of music

Musical instruments are generally divided into groups according to the main sections of an orchestra.

WOODWIND

This consists of the flute, oboe, clarinet and bassoon, and related instruments. Although flutes were originally made of wood, they are now usually made of metal, to produce a brighter sound. In addition to these main instruments, there are others of varying sizes, which produce a similar sound at different pitch ranges. The piccolo, for instance, is a small flute, with which the player is able to reach very high notes, and there is also an alto flute and even a bass flute, twice as large as an ordinary flute. The cor anglais is a larger type of oboe, and the clarinet comes in a range of different sizes, right down to the rarely-heard contrabass clarinet. The bassoon is itself quite large, but the contrabassoon is twice as big, producing deep, resonant bass notes.

Although the saxophone is made of metal, it is included in the woodwind group because its mouthpiece and fingering system are similar to the clarinet. It too is made in a range of sizes, from soprano to bass.

The recorder used to be an orchestral instrument (J. S. Bach used it in his *Brandenburg Concertos*), but nowadays it is used mainly in small groups and for solo playing. It is made in a variety of sizes, from sopranino to great bass, and its sound is soft and quite different from the flute. Wooden recorders sound more mellow than plastic ones.

10 (left) The bassoon: a "double-reed" instrument of the oboe family

11 (right) An unusual, soft-toned instrument: the bass recorder

12 The violin is the basic stringed instrument of the orchestra, and is used in many other kinds of music-making

BRASS

The horn, trumpet, trombone and tuba are often called the "heavy brass", but they are quite capable of playing softly as well as loudly. Each brass instrument has its own individual character; the horn and tuba have a more rounded tone quality, while the trumpet and trombone are brighter in tone. The system of valves enables the instruments to be used for quite fast, complicated music, although the trombone is not so agile because the player has to operate the slide. To overcome this, trombones have been made with valves, but the tone quality is not the same as the ordinary slide trombone. There is also a bass trombone, which is really a combined bass and tenor trombone, with a special valve for changing from one set of tubing to the other. In the brass band, there are several other instruments, including the cornet, tenor horn, euphonium and baritone, but they all work on the same valve system. The fact that the tubing is coiled round in a complicated way in brass instruments has no bearing on the sound; it is just to make them convenient to handle.

STRINGS

The stringed instruments normally included in the symphony orchestra are the violin, viola, cello and double-bass. Their design is the result of centuries of experience in getting just the right quality of tone combined with ease of playing. Each instrument has four strings, although some double-basses have an extra fifth string for getting down to very low notes. The strings can either be played with a bow ("arco"), or plucked with the fingers ("pizzicato") which produces a completely different kind of sound. In a symphony orchestra, the violins are usually divided into First Violins and Second Violins, but there is no difference in the actual kind of instrument used.

There is another separate family of stringed instruments, called the viols, which are not normally included in the orchestra. They produce a quieter, thinner tone than the violin family, and are used mainly in small ensembles specializing in early music. Viols are made in three main sizes: treble, tenor, and bass (the "viola da gamba").

When playing one of the violin family, the player has to judge the right place to stop the string with his finger to produce the correct note, but on the viols small lengths of gut are tied round the fingerboard to guide the player to the correct position. The same system was used on the lute, and was later made more permanent by embedding pieces of wire (or "frets") into the fingerboard to show the positions of the various notes, as on the guitar. Although this makes playing easier, it means that the player cannot make small adjustments of pitch by moving his finger-tip slightly, as he can on the violin for example.

KEYBOARDS

Although the piano-type keyboard is used to operate a variety of instruments, they do in fact work in quite different ways. In the harpsichord, the keys operate a mechanism which plucks the strings, producing a "twanging" sound. Smaller instruments which work on the same principle are the spinet and the virginals. The clavichord is a small keyboard instrument in which the strings are struck by hammers instead of being plucked: it is very quiet and useful for private practice. In the piano, the strings are also hit by hammers, but there is a special mechanism which enables them to fall away from the strings, allowing the sound to be sustained. In the organ, the keyboard is used to control the supply of air to various sets of pipes

13 A "giraffe" piano, made in Amsterdam about 1810

which can be brought into use by pulling levers called "stops". Air pressure for organs used to be produced by someone (usually a choirboy) working a set of bellows, but nowadays it is generally supplied by an electric pump, although in the case of the harmonium the player has to produce it himself by continually operating two bellows pedals while playing. The harmonium has reeds to produce the sound, rather than pipes. Another keyboard instrument is the celesta, in which soft hammers strike a series of metal bars to produce a soft, tinkling sound. The keyboard system has also been used to control recently invented instruments such as the electric piano and the synthesizer, in which the sounds are produced entirely by electronic means.

PERCUSSION

These instruments are divided into two groups: tuned and untuned. The tuned percussion produce notes of definite pitch, and in many of them, such as the xylophone, vibraphone, glockenspiel and tubular bells, the notes are arranged in a similar way to the piano keyboard. The timpani are large drums which can be tuned to particular notes by means of screw handles or adjustable pedals. The untuned percussion instruments include the side drum, bass drum, cymbals, triangle, tambourine, tam-tam, castanets, and Latin-American instruments such as the bongo drums, claves and maracas. The set of drums used in jazz and pop groups is called a "kit", and the instruments are arranged so that they can all be played by one drummer.

14 *The keyboards of a three-manual organ, showing the "stops" for producing different tone-colours*

CHAPTER FOUR

How to read music

(As this chapter contains quite a lot of information, it is best not to try to take it in all at once, but to use it for reference purposes while reading the rest of the book.)

RHYTHM

Different kinds of notes are used to show the duration of musical sounds. The most common are the crotchet (♩), minim (♩), and quaver (♪). Crotchets are often used to show each beat of the music, as in a march:

Left   right,   Left   right,   Left   right,...

or a waltz:

One   two   three, One   two   three, One   two   three, ...

To make the music easier to read, the notes are divided into groups by lines called bar-lines. Each group is called a bar, and contains a number of beats depending on the kind of music. In a march there are two beats in a bar, corresponding to the left-right rhythm of marching feet:

LEFT   right,   LEFT   right,   LEFT   right,

In a waltz there are three beats in a bar:

ONE   two   three,   ONE   two   three,   ONE   two   three,

The number of beats in each bar is shown by a "time-signature" at the beginning of the music: $\frac{2}{4}$ means that there are two beats in a bar; $\frac{3}{4}$ means three beats in a bar, etc. (the lower figure 4 shows that crotchets are being used to show the beats). $\frac{4}{4}$ means that there are four crotchets in a bar.

A minim is twice as long as a crotchet, and so lasts for two beats of the music when the beats are crotchets:

A quaver is half as long as a crotchet, and so two quavers are needed to make up one crotchet beat (the "tails" of quavers are often joined together to show this grouping: ♫). Musicians count quavers by imagining an "and" after each main beat: "one *and* two *and* three *and* four *and* . . .", etc.:

By using crotchets, minims and quavers, quite complicated patterns of rhythm can be written down:

If a dot is added to a note, its length is increased by half. So a dotted minim last for *three* crotchets instead of two, and a dotted crotchet lasts for *three* quavers. This gives even more possibilities for rhythmic variety:

Other notes often used in music are the semibreve (○), which lasts for four crotchets, and the semiquaver (♪), which lasts for a quarter of a crotchet. As with quavers, the "tails" of semiquavers are often joined together:

For every note there is also a sign for a "rest" of the same duration, for showing silence in between notes or groups of notes. The signs for rests are:

⅔ crotchet	— minim
¥ quaver	▬ semibreve
¥ semiquaver	

They are often used at the end of musical phrases:

Three blind | mice, (rest) | Three blind | mice, (rest)

The basic beat is often divided into thirds, instead of into halves and quarters, producing a different kind of "triple" rhythm. In this case, the dotted crotchet is used to show the beat, so that it can be divided into three quavers:

Half a pound of | two-pen-ny rice | Half a pound of | trea - cle

(The time-signature $\frac{6}{8}$ shows that there are six quavers in a bar, arranged into two groups of three.)

Here is an example of music using various kinds of signs:

The | grand old Duke of | York, He | had ten thou-sand | men, He

marched them up to the | top of the hill, and he | marched them down a- | gain.

PITCH

To distinguish one pitch from another, musicians call notes by the first seven letters of the alphabet: A B C D E F G. This group of letters is repeated over and over again, from the very lowest notes to the highest. On a keyboard instrument, the notes are arranged like this:

A B C D E F G, A B C D E F G, A B C D E F G, A B C D E F G, etc.

Music could be written down just by using these letter-names, but a better system is the set of five lines called a "stave" (or "staff"):

This enables the performer to see at a glance which notes are higher in pitch and which are lower. High notes are placed towards the top of the stave, and lower ones towards the bottom, and they can be placed on the lines or in the spaces, according to their pitch:

↑ high

↓ low

The exact pitches represented by the lines and spaces of the stave depend on the type of "clef" which is placed at the beginning of the stave. The most common clefs are the treble (𝄞) and the bass (𝄢), which are generally used for the right and left hands in piano music. The treble clef shows that the second line up represents the note G:

and the bass clef shows that the second line down is F:

With these notes fixed, the other notes can then be written in. (See next column.)

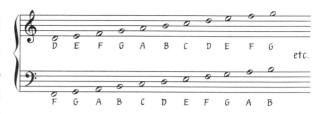

If the notes get too high or too low for the stave, "leger-lines" can be used, so that you can carry on writing notes as high or as low as you like:

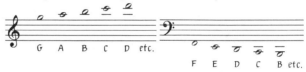

With this system, all the notes on a piano keyboard can be written on two staves:

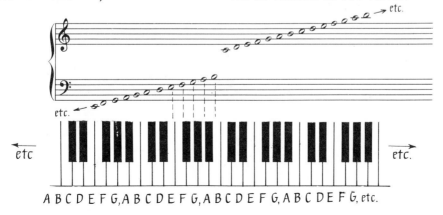

In the middle of the keyboard there is a certain amount of overlap of leger-lines: "middle C", for example, can be written either as

or as

Many simple tunes can be written down by using just the white notes on a keyboard, but for some tunes you need to use the black notes as well.

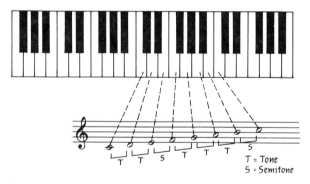

T = Tone
S = Semitone

On a keyboard, the black notes are grouped into twos and threes: this means that some pairs of white notes have a black note between them (for example G and A), but others don't (B and C, and E and F). It is this uneven grouping of the black notes which gives particular character to the "scales", or series of consecutive notes, which can be played on the white keys. Each step between notes (white *and* black) is called a "semitone", so that the pitch difference (or "interval") between B and C is one semitone, but between C and D it is two semitones (or a "tone") because there is a black note in between:

Black notes don't have letter-names themselves, but are related to the white notes on each side. The black notes are called "sharps" (♯) or "flats" (♭) according to whether they are higher or lower in pitch than the original white note, so that for example the black note between G and A can be called either G sharp or A flat, depending on the music:

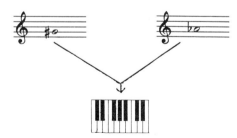

If you want to play a scale or tune higher up or lower down the keyboard (that is, if you want to "transpose" it), you will find that sharps or flats have to be used to keep the same pattern of tones and semitones, otherwise the scale will sound different from the original:

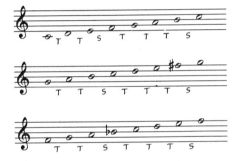

Sharps and flats are called "accidentals", and are often written at the beginning of the stave in groups called "key-signatures", which tell the player which scale (or "key") the music is based on. When an accidental appears in a key-signature, it applies to that note throughout the piece, unless it is occasionally cancelled by a "natural" sign (♮).

The pitch interval between two notes is usually described according to the number of scale steps between the notes. So, a note which is five steps up a scale is described as being a "fifth" above the starting note. The intervals of a scale are as follows:

Unison 2nd 3rd 4th 5th 6th 7th Octave

When you get to the octave, the top note sounds similar to the starting note, only higher in pitch.

In each type of scale, the intervals contain various numbers of semitones, giving the scales their individual character. For example, in a "major" scale, the "third" between the first and third notes contains four semitones, but in a "minor" scale this third contains only three semitones, making it sound quite different:

Once you have learnt the more common scales and their key-signatures, you will find that playing music of all kinds will become much easier.

CHAPTER FIVE

How music is composed

As soon as musical sounds are combined together, the skill of a composer or arranger is needed to organize them properly, so that they will sound well. If sounds clash together in a disagreeable way, they are said to be "dissonant", but if the effect is pleasant and mild, they are called "consonant". However, the best music is not all consonant—some dissonance is needed to add spice and flavour to the music, in the same way that we add salt and pepper to food to improve its taste.

HARMONY

Harmony is the resulting sound produced by two or more notes played or sung at the same time. One of its most common forms is of an accompaniment added to an existing melody, with the harmony notes formed into groups called "chords". By choosing the right chords the melody can be made more effective, and the harmony can add an extra dimension, without which the tune can sound rather plain. The harmony can also emphasize the division of the melody into phrases, by using groups of chords called "cadences" at the end of each phrase.

In the early eighteenth century, composers often used a "shorthand" system of harmonization called the "figured bass". Instead of writing out all the notes of every chord, they would simply write the lowest (or "bass") note, with figures to show the intervals of the other notes above it. Musicians knew exactly what these figures meant and could easily play the required notes, e.g.:

A similar system of "chord symbols" is used today by jazz, dance-band and pop musicians.

COUNTERPOINT

Counterpoint is the art of combining two or more melodic lines simultaneously. It is very useful in musical composition, because the addition of a counter-melody to an existing tune can add interest and provide an element of contrast. If the composer is writing one of the melodies, he can adjust it to fit the other parts, but if the melodies already exist, it is simply a matter of chance whether they fit together without causing too much dissonance. When he was writing his *Second Suite* for military band, Gustav Holst found that the traditional tunes "Greensleeves" and "The Dargason" fitted together exactly: a lucky discovery, which he also subsequently used in his *St Paul's Suite* for strings.

When one voice or instrument starts a tune, and then one or more others join in with the same tune, the result is called a "canon". A particular type of canon is the "round", in which each voice starts by singing the first phrase of the tune and then goes on to the second phrase when the next voice comes in, and so on. Familiar examples of rounds are "Three Blind Mice" and "London's Burning". Rounds can be repeated any number of times, until someone decides to call a halt. Canons and rounds are good examples of "imitation" in counterpoint, in which each part has similar music.

A more complicated type of counterpoint is the "fugue", in which the voices or instruments start off by imitating each other, but then go on to more extended passages in which the counterpoint is written freely. The writing of fugues requires considerable skill, and the composer who excelled at them was J. S. Bach, who wrote many fugues of different kinds.

FORM

When a composer has had a musical idea, he has to decide what to do with it: whether to repeat it, develop it, or perhaps "modulate" to a different key. In order to avoid the result sounding haphazard and disorganized, various musical forms have been evolved over the centuries, which composers have used in their own individual ways.

Many of the earlier instrumental forms came originally from dance music, and eighteenth-century music is full of dance movements such as the allemande, courante, bourrée, gavotte and minuet. But as instrumental music developed, composers found that these smaller forms were too limiting, and so the principle of "sonata" form was used, in which a movement could contain two or more contrasting themes which could be developed and transposed into different keys to produce a longer and more interesting structure. Sonata form was used extensively by Haydn and Mozart, and was extended by Beethoven and other nineteenth-century composers.

Other common musical forms are the "theme and variations", in which the composer can demonstrate his ability to invent all kinds of new ways of dealing with the original theme, and the "rondo", in which a particular theme keeps returning between sections of contrasting music.

ORCHESTRATION

As the orchestra developed, composers became more skilful in obtaining new and more expressive sounds from the instruments, so that orchestration eventually became an art in itself. In the world of film music today, some musicians earn their living entirely by orchestrating other composers' work. The music for an orchestra is written out in the form of a "full score", which shows the notes played by each individual instrument and how they relate to each other. A copyist then has to write out individual parts for every musician in the orchestra, so that they can see what notes they have to play. In the case of older music, these parts are often printed and can be purchased from publishers, but for unpublished music the production of a manuscript full score and complete set of parts can involve an enormous amount of work.

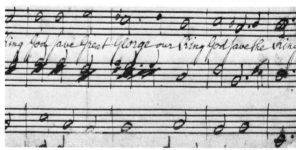

15 An early version of the British National Anthem by Thomas Augustine Arne, dating from 1745

CHAPTER SIX

Instrumental music

Musical instruments are invented sometimes in response to the needs of musicians, and sometimes according to the whim of the inventor, but composers are usually quick to take full advantage of the possibilities of any new instrument.

Before the eighteenth century, one of the most popular solo instruments was the harpsichord, with its smaller relatives the spinet and virginals. Many composers wrote music for this instrument, including the great French composers Rameau and Couperin, and the Germans Handel and J. S. Bach. But in the eighteenth century the piano was invented, and soon displaced the harpsichord in popularity, remaining one of the most widely used solo instruments up to the present day.

Most of the major composers of the last two hundred years have written music for the piano, and some, such as Chopin, made it their special instrument, almost to the exclusion of anything else. The classical composers of the late eighteenth century, such as Haydn and Mozart, wrote elegant sonatas for the earlier, less robust type of instrument, but as the design of pianos developed, composers were able to write music having a greater emotional scope and power of expression. Beethoven pioneered this approach, which was subsequently developed by composers such as Liszt and later by Rachmaninov, both of whom produced virtuoso show-pieces of great technical difficulty. In the early twentieth century, composers such as Debussy and Ravel successfully used the instrument for atmospheric impressionist music such as Debussy's *La Cathédrale Engloutie* (*The Submerged Cathedral*), and later composers have found it suitable for a wide variety of musical styles, from "neo-classicism" (see page 46) to experimental music. There is such an enormous range of piano music available that there is something to match every taste and level of ability. The piano is also very suitable for accompanying the singing voice, and was used for this purpose with great effect by romantic composers such as Schubert and Schumann. In the nineteenth century no middle-class home was complete without its parlour piano, round which the family would gather to sing songs in the evenings.

But perhaps too much emphasis has been placed on learning the piano in the past, and recently some musicians have shown that other instruments can be very effective in a solo role. This is particularly true of the classical guitar, which has risen from a mere accompaniment instrument to become a solo instrument in its own right, through the work of virtuoso players such as Andrés Segovia and John Williams. The popularity of Rodrigo's *Concierto de Aranjuez* has shown that the guitar can be an effective solo instrument with the orchestra, in the right setting. The guitar is also ideal for accompanying songs, as was the lute in Elizabethan times.

Practically all the instruments mentioned in Chapter 3 have had solo music written for them, often with keyboard accompaniment. This means that whatever instrument you may decide to take up, you will find that there is a wide range of music available, including scales and exercises to improve your technical ability. But however interesting playing a solo instrument can be, it is not so much fun as playing in a group with other people, which is a different kind of experience altogether.

In the Elizabethan period, many households had sets of instruments available so that guests could play together after dinner. These instruments were generally viols or recorders, and a group of the same type was called a "consort". If the instruments were of different kinds, it was called a "broken consort". Many great composers of the time wrote music for amateur musicians to play, including William Byrd, Thomas Morley, and Orlando Gibbons. In the Restoration period Henry Purcell wrote some fine fantasias for viols when he was at the beginning of his career.

In the twentieth century, the use of these early instruments has been revived, particularly the recorder, which has become popular through the work of the Dolmetsch family. Perhaps the best kind of recorder group to play in is a quartet of descant, treble, tenor and bass, which can produce a rich, resonant sound quite different from a school recorder class playing with piano accompaniment.

16 A recorder ensemble, in which anyone can join, regardless of age

In the seventeenth century, these consorts of instruments gave way to the "trio sonata", which, confusingly, is neither a trio nor a sonata. It requires four players: two melody instruments, such as violins, flutes or oboes, a keyboard (harpsichord or organ) and a bass instrument (cello or bassoon). The word "sonata" is used in its original sense of meaning simply "sound", rather than the sonata form of the later classical composers. Also during this period the viols were supplanted by the violin family, mainly because these newer instruments provided a more powerful sound for use in opera and symphonic music. But the violin family was also quite suitable for small-scale music-making, and by the end of the eighteenth century the string quartet was a well-established combination, consisting of two violins, viola and cello. Many amateurs played in string quartets for their own enjoyment, and composers wrote music in which the parts provided something of interest for each player but also interwove with each other, so that the result was rather like an interesting conversation for four people. The first great composers of string quartets were Haydn and Mozart, who were followed in the nineteenth century by Beethoven, Schubert, Mendelssohn and Brahms.

In the twentieth century, composers such as Bartok and Shostakovich have used the string quartet for the expression of profound musical ideas, but their works are difficult to play and are more likely to be performed by professionals than by amateurs.

18 Trumpets can be played in small brass ensembles, brass and military bands, and the full symphony orchestra

Small-scale music-making for the players' own enjoyment is called "chamber music", and besides the string quartet there are many other combinations, including the string quintet (string quartet plus an extra viola or cello), the string trio (violin,

17 A string quartet consists of two violins, a viola and a cello

19 The full range of saxophones, from the soprano (right) to the bass (left)

viola and cello), the piano quintet (piano plus string quartet), piano quartet (piano and string trio) and piano trio (piano, violin and cello). Wind instruments are often included in chamber music, joining with the strings in groups such as the clarinet quintet (clarinet with string quartet) and the oboe quartet (oboe with string trio). A group consisting entirely of wind instruments is the wind quintet, which consists of flute, oboe, clarinet, bassoon and horn, covering a wide range of pitch with a contrasting mixture of tone-colours, so that it is almost like a small wind orchestra in itself.

Playing chamber music demands a high standard of musicianship, but the pleasure of playing with other people makes the effort of learning an instrument really worth while. Even playing in a simple recorder group with some friends can provide a worthwhile and enjoyable musical experience, and there are no barriers of age or background—anyone who can play an instrument can join in.

CHAPTER SEVEN

Orchestral music

In the seventeenth century, or "Baroque" period, the orchestra as we know it today began to take shape. At first it consisted mainly of stringed instruments: both King Louis XIV of France and King Charles II of England had orchestras of 24 strings to play for their entertainment. These orchestras also generally included a harpsichord which provided a "continuo" accompaniment of chords from a figured bass (see Chapter 5). In this period one of the most common forms of orchestral music was the "concerto grosso", in which a small group of soloists (the "concertino") was contrasted with the rest of the orchestra (the "ripieno"). Perhaps the best-known works in this form are the six *Brandenburg Concertos* by J. S. Bach, which have also parts for a variety of instruments.

During the eighteenth century, wind instruments became regular members of the orchestra, and the continuo gradually disappeared, so that by the end of the century an orchestra would usually consist of two flutes, two oboes, two clarinets, two bassoons, two horns, two trumpets, timpani and strings, which remains the usual basic orchestral combination to the present day. Coupled with the evolution of the orchestra was the development of the symphony, which resulted from the work of C. P. E. Bach (one of the sons of J. S. Bach), whose ideas were developed and expanded by Haydn and Mozart. The form of the symphony was related to that of the string quartet and piano sonata, and had its origins in the earlier Italian style of overture, which was in three sections: fast, slow, and fast. By the end of Haydn's life the symphony had come to be a work in four movements, the first of which was usually a fast movement in sonata form, the second slow, the third a minuet, and the fourth often a lively rondo. This period is called the "Classical" period in musical history because of its well-proportioned forms and the elegance of its musical language.

20 *The double-bass, largest instrument of the string family*

There were also numerous concertos in which a single soloist (rather than the "concertino" of the Baroque period) was set against the full orchestra. Composers often gave the soloist a chance to improvise his own music by providing space for a "cadenza" in which the orchestra remained silent while the soloist could display his abilities in brilliant passage-work.

The work of the Classical composers was developed by Beethoven, who turned the symphony into a longer and more substantial type of composition. He substituted a "scherzo" for the previous minuet, and extended the relationships between keys, so that the music could modulate through a wider range of keys during the course of a movement. He also made more demands on the players, who had to extend their instrumental technique, and manufacturers began to think of ways of improving the design of instruments so that they could be more versatile. During the nineteenth century valves were added to horns and trumpets, and systems of levers and pads were applied to woodwind instruments, making them more agile than their eighteenth-century predecessors. This enabled composers to write more complex and exciting music for the orchestra, and "Romantic" composers such as Berlioz and

Wagner exploited the expressive possibilities of the full orchestra to the utmost.

21 The soft tone of the horns gives a characteristic colour to the sound of the orchestra

Some Romantic composers continued the development of the symphony, while others invented completely new forms such as the "symphonic poem" (or "tone-poem") which could be used to tell a story in music—this is often called "programme music". Examples are the *Symphonie Fantastique* by Berlioz, and Tchaikovsky's *Francesca da Rimini* which tells a love story in music.

The solo concerto was also extended and developed in the nineteenth century, and was an ideal form for the ideas of Romantic composers, who often saw the individual creative artist (the soloist) as being someone apart from, and sometimes in conflict with, the rest of society (the orchestra). Developments in the design of the piano made it a much more powerful instrument than in the Classical period, enabling it to compete with the full orchestra on its own terms.

It was at this time that the art of conducting came into being. In the Baroque and Classical periods, orchestras were directed either by the first violinist (the "leader") or from the harpsichord. In the nineteenth century conducting an orchestra became an art in itself, and nowadays it is a very specialized branch of musical activity.

By the end of the nineteenth century and the early years of the twentieth century, composers were writing for very large orchestras, often including three or more of each type of woodwind instrument, with large brass sections, percussion, and strings to match. Richard Strauss and Gustav Mahler used such orchestras, and twentieth-century composers such as Schoenberg, Stravinsky, Bartok and Prokofiev started off by using very large orchestras, particularly for ballet music. But after the First World War, composers turned to smaller orchestral combinations, partly for financial reasons, and partly because of a growing revival of interest in music of the Classical period. Many composers started to write music based on the style and forms of the eighteenth century, producing a new style known as "Neo-Classicism", of which Igor Stravinsky was perhaps the best-known exponent.

Nowadays, professional orchestras play mainly music from the last two hundred years, as the cost of rehearsing and performing new works is enormous, but amateur orchestras get a great deal of pleasure from playing music of all periods, provided that it is within their technical ability.

There are other kinds of orchestral groups besides the symphony orchestra. In Britain, particularly in the North of England, there is a strong tradition of brass band music, which is played mainly by amateur musicians. Very high standards are achieved, and bands compete against each other every year for a trophy at the National Brass Band Championships. Another type of orchestra is the wind band, which is similar to the brass band but with the addition of woodwind instruments. In Britain, the wind band has been mainly associated with military music, but in the USA there is a great interest in wind music, particularly among young people, and wind bands are

22 *The oboe: an important member of the woodwind section*

found in many colleges and high schools, playing arrangements of symphonic music or compositions specially written for the band. The wind band is particularly suitable for amateur players, as it is possible to achieve a high standard of performance in rather less time than is normally needed for stringed instruments.

23 *The tuba, often called the "bass" in brass and military bands*

CHAPTER EIGHT

Vocal music

Music has been made with the human voice from the earliest times, as it is the cheapest musical instrument of all, and is owned by everyone!

Voices are grouped into male and female, and are often referred to by letters such as S, A, T and B, standing for Soprano, Alto, Tenor and Bass. The ranges of voices are approximately as follows:

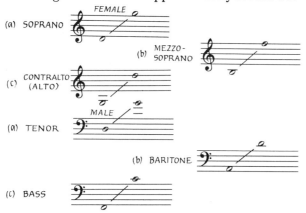

To avoid the use of too many leger-lines, music for the tenor voice is usually written an octave higher than it sounds, using a treble clef with a figure 8 below it to show that the sounds are an octave lower than written:

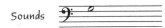

Vocal music has always been particularly associated with the church, and some of the earliest surviving music is the Christian chant called Gregorian chant, named after Pope Gregory the Great. Gregorian chant consists entirely of melody—there is no harmony—and has its own particularly kind of rhythm which is not divided up by bar-lines but flows along freely from phrase to phrase.

In later centuries, musicians discovered the art of combining voices to produce harmony and counterpoint. At first harmony was made by a rather simple system called "organum", but gradually composers discovered how to write more complex music while still remaining within the capabilities of the human voice. By the time of Palestrina in the sixteenth century, vocal composition had reached a high level, and composers throughout Europe were writing music for voices with great skill. The main forms of church music were the Mass and the Motet, both using Latin words, and these were sung by trained singers in church choirs. The Mass was a musical setting of the Communion service, and the motet was a separate composition, often based on words from the Bible. After the Reformation in the sixteenth century, composers started to write music for the Protestant churches, using the ordinary language of the people, instead of Latin. Hymns were written using familiar "chorale" melodies so that the congregation could join in the singing, while the Anthem served the same sort of purpose as the motet in the Catholic service.

In the Baroque and Classical periods, composers started to make more use of instruments as well as voices in church music, and new forms such as the Oratorio and Cantata were developed. Perhaps the most famous church cantatas are those of J. S. Bach, which cover the whole of the church year and are scored for various combinations of soloists, chorus, and instrumental forces. Bach also wrote two large-scale cantatas, the *St Matthew Passion* and the *St John Passion*, which are based on the Gospels according to St Matthew and St John. The best-known oratorio is probably Handel's *Messiah*, also based on the Bible, which was first performed in Dublin and has since been performed thousands of times throughout the world. Towards the end of the eighteenth century, orchestras were often used with voices even in settings of the Mass, making it seem more like a large-scale cantata or oratorio, with soloists singing in operatic style.

In the nineteenth century, particularly in England, cantatas and oratorios were sung by very large choirs, sometimes numbering thousands of people, but this fashion for large-scale singing died out during the twentieth century. On a smaller scale of composition, many hymns and carols were written in the eighteenth and nineteenth centuries, and remain familiar to the present day.

Music which is not religious is called "secular"

music, and a great deal of secular vocal music has survived from previous centuries. In Elizabethan times, educated people were expected to be able to join in singing after dinner, as well as play musical instruments. The main form of secular vocal music at that time was the "madrigal", which originated in Italy, but also became very popular in England. The words were often not very serious, and included meaningless syllables such as "fa la la la la la . . ." The music involved a great deal of interplay between the parts, so that the madrigal was really a kind of vocal chamber music. Madrigals were published in part-books, so that a singer could buy a book containing the music for his own type of voice (scores were rarely printed). Sometimes the parts for madrigals were printed all on one page, but facing in different directions, so that the book could be placed on a table and used by several singers at the same time. Some well-known composers of madrigals were the Englishmen Byrd, Morley, Weelkes and Wilbye, and on the continent Marenzio, Rore and Lassus.

The custom of singing madrigals declined in the Baroque period, but in eighteenth-century England a new form of small-scale secular vocal music appeared: the Glee. Glee singing was confined to male singers and was generally performed in public houses, where regular meetings of glee-clubs would take place. The words of the glees are very light, often in praise of drinking, and the music sometimes even has special rests written into the parts so that the singers can have a chance to drink their beer! Glee-clubs also sang rounds (or "catches") and many well-known composers wrote this entertaining music.

24 *"The Concert": a painting by Lorenzo Costa (1460–1530)*

In the nineteenth century, part-songs were written for amateurs to sing, and these included female as well as male voices, often with piano accompaniment. Although these part-songs were not so complex musically as the Elizabethan madrigals, they gave the performers much pleasure to sing.

25 *A round, or "rota", sung by men in eighteenth-century glee clubs*

the popularity of amateur vocal music, but increasing numbers of people are re-discovering that it is much more enjoyable to join in something oneself than listen to someone else doing it. Even people who are not specialist musicians can get great pleasure from singing in a choir if they are prepared to work as part of a team, and many have discovered the richness of the vocal music of previous centuries in this way.

26 *Singing in a school choir can be rewarding—for teachers as well as for pupils!*

In the twentieth century, the rise of radio, television and recordings has done much to diminish

Many people also enjoy singing in amateur operatic societies. Opera was invented in Italy at the beginning of the seventeenth century, and the works of Monteverdi are the best-known surviving from that period today. Many of the early operas were based on legends and mythology, and were designed to show off the voices of the singers. In the later eighteenth century, composers such as Mozart and Haydn developed the art of opera, and used their musical skill to portray human characters and express their emotions in music. The Romantic composers of the nineteenth century used all the possibilities of opera to produce overwhelming effects: particularly Wagner, who aimed at combining the work of the author, composer, and designer into a new kind of art. Also in the nineteenth century the art of operetta emerged: a light style of opera which is easy to listen to and pleasurable to sing. The works of Gilbert and Sullivan are perhaps the best known in this category in Britain today.

The nineteenth-century Italian operatic tradition of Donizetti and Verdi was carried on into the twentieth century by Puccini, but fewer operas are written today compared with previous centuries. In Britain, Benjamin Britten made a particular success of writing operas to English words.

CHAPTER NINE

Folk music

Throughout the centuries, ordinary people have made their own music quite separately from the "art" music which was composed for and listened to by educated people. Because peasants or farm workers could not usually read or write, this music was rarely written down, but was passed on by ear from one generation to the next. This meant that each person added a little of his own character to the music, as it is difficult to pass on something verbally without making some changes, however much you try to be accurate. A good example of this process is the story of soldiers passing a message along a trench by word of mouth. What started off as: "Send reinforcements, we're going to advance" ended up at the end of the trench as: "Send three-and-fourpence, we're going to a dance"!

Each part of Britain has produced its own characteristic folk music, particularly Scotland and Ireland, where traditional music is still widely appreciated. But in England, the Industrial Revolution of the nineteenth century drew large numbers of people away from the land and into the cities to work in factories, so that the folk music associated with the agricultural seasons of the year began to disappear. Then at the beginning of the twentieth century some musicians discovered that folk-songs were still being sung in various parts of the country, and they set out to collect as many songs as possible before they vanished completely. Musicians such as Cecil Sharp, Ralph Vaughan Williams and Percy Grainger toured the country in the early 1900s, persuading people to sing folk-songs so that they could write them down. Some of these collectors recorded the songs they heard on wax-cylinder recording machines, although the singers were often suspicious of this new-fangled invention.

The collectors of English folk-songs found that the music had its own special kind of beauty, with a freedom of melody and flexibility of rhythm reminiscent of the flowing character of Gregorian chant. Here is one of the first songs collected by Ralph Vaughan Williams, "Bushes and Briars", which he heard sung by an old man at Ingrave in Essex in 1903:

Many of the songs seemed to be unaffected by the developments in harmony which had taken place in the last few hundred years, and were often sung without any harmonic accompaniment at all. Some of the collectors tried to compose piano accompaniments to fit the songs, but found that this wasn't always easy. The reason for this is that many of the melodies are not in the modern key system, but are in the older system of "modes", which are the scales produced by playing only on the white notes of a keyboard without using any black notes. Each mode has its own character,

according to the note used as the starting-point, and is given a special name, some of which are as follows:

Cecil Sharp even pursued English folk music as far away as the USA, where he found survivals of English folk-songs among the people of the Appalachian Mountains. After this period of intense activity by the early collectors there was something of a lull. Then after the Second World War interest in folk music revived in Britain, and there are now folk-music clubs meeting regularly all over the country, devoted to keeping the music of the various regions alive. Folk singers also appear at large-scale concerts which attract big audiences, providing quite a different setting from the atmosphere of the traditional village pub.

There has also been an increase of interest by Westerners in the music of India and the Orient. Some countries do not have the division between "art" music and "folk" music which is generally found in Europe. In India, for example, the musical tradition stretches back over thousands of years, and reached a high level many centuries ago. The training of Indian musicians is very strict, and they have to learn many scales or "ragas" by heart. These ragas are quite different from the scales of Western music, often containing intervals of less than a semitone, and they are intended to express different kinds of emotion, or to be played at particular times of the day or night. None of the music is written down, and the player has to learn by ear and develop a skill in improvisation, an art which has almost disappeared from European music. One of the commonest Indian instruments is the Sitar, a stringed instrument played by plucking, with special strings to provide resonating notes. Also very important to Indian music is the rhythm or "tala", which is often

27 *Russell Wortley, a traditional English performer on the pipe and tabor*

played on a drum called the "tabla". Many of the rhythms are much more complex than the familiar two, three, or four beats-in-the-bar of Western music, and this is one of the things which makes Indian music so fascinating.

28 *Ravi Shankar, master of the Indian sitar*

29 *A drummer of a gamelang orchestra on the island of Bali*

Percussion is also very important in the music of other oriental countries, particularly China and Japan, where the five-note (or "pentatonic") scale is also widely used. In the island of Bali in Indonesia, whole orchestras are made up of percussion instruments resembling xylophones and glockenspiels of various sizes, with sets of gongs and chimes. This Balinese "gamelang" music has had an important influence on certain European composers, particularly Claude Debussy, who heard the Balinese musicians at the Paris Exposition of 1889, and the contemporary French composer Pierre Boulez. Percussion instruments have been used extensively in recent compositions by many Western composers, who have discovered new and subtle possibilities in the use of percussive sounds from the example of oriental music.

Instead of being used simply as a reinforcement for rhythmic patterns, the orchestral percussion section is now regarded as an independent group, on the same basis as the strings, woodwind and brass. Some composers, such as Edgard Varèse and Carlos Chávez, have even written entire works for ensembles of percussion instruments, but it is in conjunction with the sounds of other types of instrument that the percussion is perhaps at its best.

30 Gheorghe Zamfir: a popular performer on the Romanian pan-pipes

CHAPTER TEN

Jazz and pop

In recent years the barriers between "serious" and "popular" music have been worn down. At one time, it would have been unthinkable for a "classical" musician to play jazz, but nowadays musicians often move freely between these different forms of music-making, each of which demands its own particular skill. For example, the classical guitarist John Williams formed the pop group "Sky" in 1978, while jazz-based composers such as John Dankworth are equally at home with film music and "serious" composition.

The origins of jazz and pop lie in the music of the Negro slaves of America: the effect of European influences on their own traditional African music produced some completely new musical forms such as the Negro spiritual and the blues. When the opposing armies were disbanded at the end of the American Civil War, a large number of cheap military instruments came on to the market, and these later formed the basis of the first jazz bands of New Orleans at the beginning of the twentieth century. These bands usually consisted of a "front line" of trumpet (or cornet), clarinet and trombone, backed up by a "rhythm section" of piano (or banjo), bass and drums.

All this early jazz was played "by ear", as few of the musicians could read music, but they developed extraordinary skill in improvising around a basic theme, an essential ingredient of jazz, giving it vitality and immediacy, with the result that no two performances are exactly alike. The other important ingredient of jazz is the "swing" provided by the rhythm section, and the interplay between the improvised parts and this steady beat produces the same kind of tension as the rhythmic displacement, or "syncopation", used by earlier musicians such as the Elizabethan madrigal composers.

31 Sky: the popular group founded by the classical guitarist John Williams

The "traditional" jazz of the early years soon developed into other types, such as those associated with the particular locations of Chicago or Kansas City, and composers soon started to try their hand at writing down jazz in the form of arrangements or original compositions for larger groups of musicians, or "big bands". Jazz compositions which are entirely written down are apt to sound rather stilted and artificial, because the essential element of improvisation is missing, so the most successful jazz composers, such as Duke Ellington and Count Basie, allowed sufficient time in their compositions for individual musicians to improvise a "solo". The solo part would contain a set of chord symbols to give the player an outline of the harmony on which to base his improvisation—a system rather similar to the figured bass harmonizations of the eighteenth century. Many jazz compositions are based on a twelve-bar, or "blues" theme, while others follow the thirty-two bar pattern found in many popular songs. The harmonic outline of these forms is repeated over and over again while the improvisations take place, so that the form of most jazz compositions resembles the "theme and variations" of European music.

32 A set of chord symbols for a twelve-bar "blues" chorus

After the Second World War, a new movement called "bebop" appeared in jazz, in which the themes, harmonies and rhythms became much more complex than before, and jazz lost its "happy-go-lucky" atmosphere. Jazz musicians began to take their art much more seriously, and within a few years jazz evolved in a similar way to "serious" music, becoming more experimental and more removed from popular taste, so that some contemporary jazz improvisation is scarcely distinguishable from the results produced by "classical" improvisation groups. Jazz has therefore followed the same line of development as "serious" music, from primitive origins to an experimental avant-garde, but in a much shorter period of time, being compressed entirely into the twentieth century.

Luckily, the short history of jazz has coincided almost exactly with the development of sound recording, so that the improvisations of most of the great jazz performers have been preserved on record. What would we give to be able to listen to recordings of the improvisations of Bach, Mozart, or Beethoven!

The gap in public demand left by jazz when it became more obscure was quickly filled by pop music, which has now developed into an enormous and diverse field of musical activity, and the appreciation of jazz has dwindled into a minority taste. But the influence of jazz can still be heard in pop music: the rhythm section of guitar, bass and drums is basically the same as in jazz, and the solo improvisations of pop guitarists are heavily influenced by the playing of jazz musicians and of the early Negro blues singers, who attempted to imitate the sound of the human voice with their instruments.

33 The electric bass guitar: this instrument has no frets on the fingerboard, giving the player greater freedom of pitch

34 Barbara Thompson, who leads her own group "Paraphernalia", playing the alto saxophone

The development of pop music has been heavily influenced by electronic technology, which has transformed the simple guitar sound almost out of recognition. The invention of electronic synthesizers has meant that a wide range of completely new sounds is now available to pop musicians, both in the recording studio and in stage performances, where amplification has reached levels of power undreamt of a generation ago.

But in spite of all these technical developments, it is musical imagination, invention and skill which produce the most lasting results, as with any other kind of music, and pop music in which these qualities appear, such as the songs of The Beatles, has outlasted many uninspired imitations and has given great pleasure to millions of people throughout the world.

CHAPTER ELEVEN

Sound recording

35 An early disc gramophone, dating from 1903

During the last hundred years, the recording and reproduction of sound has developed from a primitive curiosity into a complex technological process. The first recordings were made on wax cylinders, which were soon replaced by discs similar to those in use today, the turntable speed being subsequently standardized at 78 revolutions per minute (r.p.m.). Later developments in plastics enabled the long-playing record to be produced, with a quieter surface and longer playing time (at $33\frac{1}{3}$ r.p.m.), and also the familiar seven-inch "single" (45 r.p.m.).

At first recordings were made acoustically, with performers playing or singing into a large horn attached to the groove-cutting machine, but later an electrical method was invented in which several microphones could be used to pick up the sounds of the instruments and the resulting "mixed" sound fed into an electrical cutting machine. All these early recordings had to be made one side at a time, and if anything went wrong the whole side had to be recorded again. The invention of the tape recorder changed all that, and mistakes could be left in the recording, to be cut out later when the tape was finally "edited". The music could also be recorded in much shorter sections, and joined together at a later stage. All modern recordings are made on to tape first and then transferred on to disc when the editing is complete. The invention of stereo recording, using two "channels" of sound instead of one, made for greater realism, and subsequent development of quadraphonic (four-channel) and multi-track (many-channel) recording has changed the art of sound recording out of all recognition.

Studios for sound recording are divided into two main sections: the studio itself, which has specially treated walls and acoustic screens, and the control room, where the producer and sound engineer sit. The control room contains all the recording equipment and is insulated from the studio so that the sound of the machines will not come out on the recording, but the producer and engineer can speak to the musicians in the studio through a special microphone and loudspeaker. The outputs from all the microphones in the studio are taken through to a large mixing desk in the control room, where a balance of sound can be obtained by adjusting the controls for each channel. The people in the control room can hear the

36 A Studer 24-track tape recorder, which uses two-inch-wide tape

resulting sound through "monitor" loudspeakers, so that the final balance can be adjusted until it satisfies them. The musicians in the studio cannot normally hear this while recording, but they can put on headphones and listen to a special "fold-back" of the resulting sound.

37 The view from the control room into the studio

In addition to balancing the sound, the engineer can add effects such as artificial echo before the music is recorded on tape, so that the result may be quite different from the sounds actually produced in the studio. After adjustments have been made to the microphone positions while the musicians run through the music, a recording or "take" is made, usually on to a multi-track machine on which as many as sixteen, twenty-four, or even more strands or "tracks" of music can be recorded. These tracks are often not all recorded at the same time, and some musicians who appear together on records may never have seen each other in the studio, having simply recorded their own contribution on to a track in time with the music already recorded on other tracks. When the recording is complete, all the tracks are combined, or "mixed-down", into the two stereo tracks needed for the usual disc or cassette.

Although domestic tape recorders are not so complicated or expensive as those used in professional studios, the basic principles are the same. The sound is recorded on to plastic tape which has been coated with a magnetic powder: this passes in front of "heads" which transfer the sound on to the tape—an "erase" head to clean the tape of any previous recordings, and record and playback heads, which are often combined. Most machines have switches for different tape speeds: the faster speeds give better quality sound and should be used for recording music, while the lower speeds are suitable only for speech. The size and shape of the room and also its furnishings all have an effect on the recordings, so it is worth experimenting with different microphone positions before making a recording. A bare room will sound harsh and echoing, while a heavily-furnished room will make the recording sound dull and muffled. It is a good idea to use a room facing away from the street, otherwise traffic noises may come out on the recording.

It is quite easy to edit tape yourself, using a "reel-to-reel" tape recorder (cassettes are much more difficult to edit). All you need is a single-edged razor-blade, an editing block and some special splicing tape (do not use ordinary sticky tape, as the glue will make the tape stick to the heads). Editing can also be done with a pair of scissors, but make sure that they are not magnet-ized, otherwise a click will be produced on the tape. Mark the place where you want to cut the tape with a yellow chinagraph pencil, and cut it in the diagonal groove of the editing block. To join two pieces of tape together, put the diagonal ends

38 Tape editing: note the music score in front of the editor

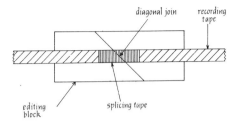

39 Splicing a tape, using an editing block and special adhesive tape

into the block so that they just touch, and stick a piece of splicing tape over them, making sure that it does not project beyond the width of the tape. With some practice, a certain amount of skill in editing tape can be achieved, so that you can join together sections of different recordings, change the order of sounds on a tape, or build up completely new compositions in sound, as described in the next chapter.

CHAPTER TWELVE

Electronic music

Although electrical musical instruments such as the electric organ had been developed in the first part of the twentieth century, it was not until the invention of the tape recorder that electronic music came into its own. Previously, sounds could be recorded directly on to gramophone records, but magnetic tape is a much more flexible medium, and can easily be cut and re-joined to get rid of unwanted sounds, or to bring together the best parts of several "takes" of a recording session.

At first, tape recorders were used simply to record musical performances or other sounds, and then composers realized that they could also be used creatively by manipulating the tape in various ways. It was thought that "perfect" performances of conventional music could be produced in this way, thus eliminating the "unreliable" human performer, but the amount of labour involved in assembling very large numbers of small pieces of tape and joining them together to make the finished product made this idea too daunting. Instead, composers started to experiment with completely new sounds, without attempting to imitate older music. They recorded sounds from various sources, such as electronic oscillators or simple everyday sounds such as the clatter of knives and forks or dustbin lids, and subjected them to various processes such as speeding them up, slowing them down, playing them backwards, or adding echo. You can try some of these things for yourself on an ordinary domestic tape recorder: if you record a voice or instrument at a high speed and play it back at low speed, it will sound quite different, and vice versa. Another interesting thing to do is to record a sound, cut out that particular section of tape, and splice it into a loop. When this loop is played back on the tape recorder, the sound will repeat over and over again, rather like the "ostinato" effect in conventional music. The frequency of repetition will depend on the size of the loop and the playback speed.

40 *A large electronic music synthesizer, capable of generating a wide range of sounds*

When these new sounds were first produced, a distinction was made between "electronic music", which was produced entirely from electronic equipment, and "musique concrète", which was based on the sounds of objects such as tin cans, human voices, or existing musical instruments. Nowdays, these distinctions are no longer made, and recently the term "electro-acoustic music" has been used to describe all the possible types of electronic music, including the use of electronic oscillators or ordinary sounds as source material, electronic modification of the sounds of conventional musical instruments, pre-recorded or "live" performances of electronic music, and playing a musical instrument to the accompaniment of a pre-recorded electronic "backing" tape.

In the last twenty years a tremendous variety of special equipment for electronic music has been developed, so that processes which took the first experimenters hours to carry out can now be done in a fraction of a second. It is no longer necessary to cut up pieces of tape containing recordings of sounds and then splice them together again; the required sounds can all be stored in a computer and then re-generated when needed. The electronic oscillators of the early days have been replaced by synthesizers, which can produce a wide range of basic tones which are then modified in various ways to produce a bewildering variety of sounds, many of which cannot be produced by conventional musical instruments. By combining synthesizers, computers, and modern multi-track recording techniques, an enormous range of possibilities has been opened up for the production of electronic music. It has even become possible at last to produce those so-called "perfect" performances of classical music dreamt of in the early years of electronic music, and although these remain rather "electronic" in sound and do not attempt to imitate the tone-colours of the original instruments, they have succeeded in bringing an

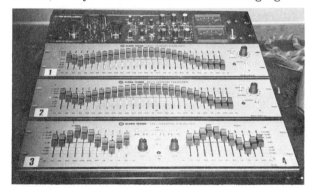

41 Graphic equalizers, used for controlling the sound level of different pitches

42 Noise-limiting units, used in sound recording and electronic music

appreciation of classical music to much wider audiences who would normally never listen to such music.

Although there have been many technological developments in electronic music, interesting and original work can still be produced using simple methods, and the work of the first electronic composers, such as Pierre Henry and Pierre Schaeffer, still stands up well beside more recent productions. It is not necessary to have an expensive electronic studio to enjoy making this kind of music yourself. Very effective results can be produced with ordinary tape recorders, provided you are prepared to take the time and trouble to build up a complete composition from very small elements. Also, the production of electronic music does not require a knowledge of the theory of music, or of electronics for that matter, and so can be used creatively by anyone who has not learned a musical instrument or is unable to do so.

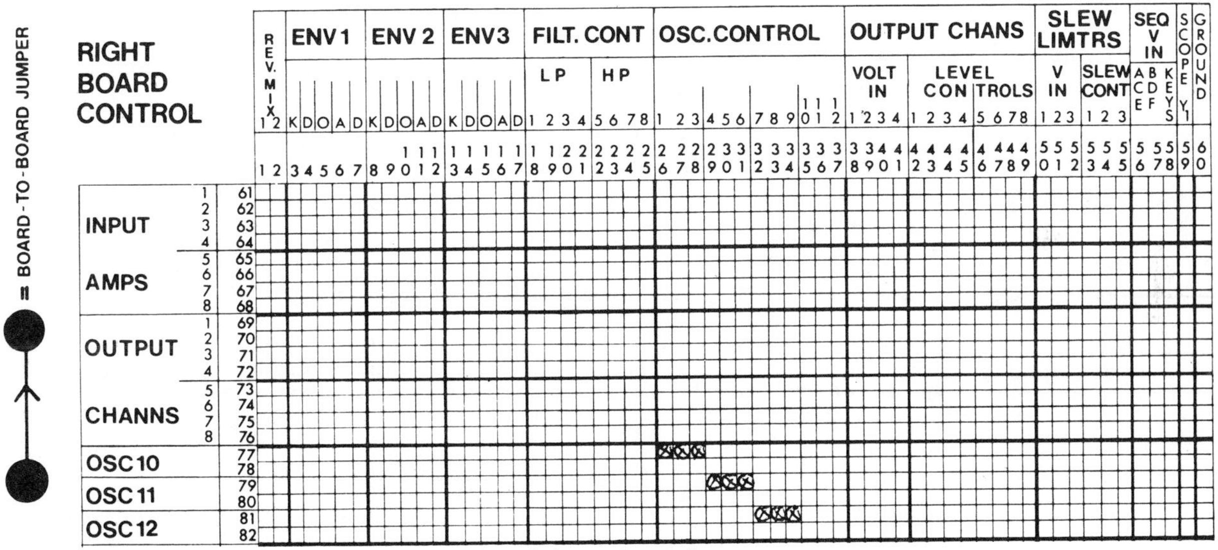
= BOARD-TO-BOARD JUMPER
RIGHT BOARD CONTROL
REV. MIX
ENV 1
ENV 2
ENV3
FILT. CONT
LP
HP
OSC.CONTROL
OUTPUT CHANS
VOLT IN
LEVEL CONTROLS
SLEW LIMTRS
V IN
SLEW CONT
SEQ V IN
SCOPE
GROUND
KEYS
INPUT
AMPS
OUTPUT
CHANNS
OSC 10
OSC 11
OSC 12

43 A "patching" chart, used in the composition of electronic music

LEARNING AN INSTRUMENT

If you decide to take up an instrument, the first important thing to do is to find a good teacher. If you start off by teaching yourself you could get into bad habits which may be difficult to get rid of later on. Perhaps the best way of finding a teacher is to ask someone whose playing you admire to give you lessons, but if this is not possible, your public library may have a list of local music teachers or may be able to show you the list of teachers published by the Incorporated Society of Musicians. When learning an instrument, you can take the graded examinations of the Associated Board of the Royal Schools of Music, as this gives you something to work towards, but examinations should never become an end in themselves—it is the music which is most important, and the pleasure of music-making should never be marred by academic considerations.

MUSIC AS A CAREER

If you would like to take up music as a career you should seek the advice of your teacher as soon as possible, as your training will depend on the type of career you intend to follow. For players of orchestral instruments who have achieved a high standard, the county youth orchestras can provide an excellent opportunity of obtaining performing experience, and there are some schools, such as the Purcell School and the Menuhin School, which specialize in preparing young people for a musical career. When you leave school, your training will be continued at one of the colleges of music, or perhaps at a university; again, it is essential to obtain advice before committing yourself to any particular course of study. A book entitled *Training and Careers for the Professional Musician* by Gerald McDonald (Unwin, 1979) may help in deciding on the best kind of career, but you must always bear in mind that the life of a professional musician can be difficult and precarious, and only the most talented and determined are likely to succeed.

MUSICAL TERMS

Musicians often use Italian words or abbreviations to give instructions as to how to perform music. Here are some of the more common terms:

Accel (accelerando)	Getting faster
Ad lib (ad libitum)	Freely
Adagio	Slow
Allegretto	Fairly fast
Allegro	Fast
Andante	Moderately
Cresc (crescendo)	Getting louder
D.C. (da capo)	Repeat from the beginning
D.S. (dal segno)	Repeat from the sign 𝄌
Dim (diminuendo)	Getting softer
Dolce	Sweetly
Fine	The end (after a "da capo" section)
Largo	Broad
Legato	Smoothly
Leggiero	Lightly
Lento	Slow
Maestoso	Majestically
Marcato	Marked
Meno	Less
Moderato	Moderately
Morendo	Dying away
Mosso	Moved (e.g. meno mosso: slower, più mosso: faster)
Non	Not
Pesante	Heavy
Poco	A little
Presto	Very fast
Più	More
Rall (rallentando)	Slowing down
Rit (ritardando)	Holding back (slowing down)
Sempre	Always
Senza	Without
Sim (simile)	The same
Stacc (staccato)	Detached notes
Sub (subito)	Suddenly
Troppo	Too much
Vivace	Lively
Vivo	Lively
Volti	Turn over the page

Dynamics

The loudness of a piece of music is shown by the following series of letters and signs:

ff (fortissimo)	Very loud
f (forte)	Loud
mf (mezzo-forte)	Moderately loud
mp (mezzo-piano)	Moderately soft
p (piano)	Soft
pp (pianissimo)	Very soft
————————	Getting louder
————————	Getting softer
sfz (sforzando)	Forced (accented)
> ∧	Accents

SUGGESTIONS FOR FURTHER READING

An ABC of Music. Imogen Holst. Oxford University Press

The New Penguin Dictionary of Music. Arthur Jacobs. Penguin Books

Introducing Music. Ottó Károlyi. Penguin Books

Tune. Imogen Holst. Faber and Faber. (This is now out of print, but can probably be obtained through a public library.)

Musical Instruments of the West. Mary Remnant. Batsford

Instruments of the Orchestra. John Hosier. Oxford University Press

Your Book of the Guitar. Graham Wade. Faber and Faber

Your Book of the Recorder. John M. Thomson. Faber and Faber

Jazz: an Introduction to its Musical Basis. Avril Dankworth. Oxford University Press

Composing with Tape Recorders. Terence Dwyer. Oxford University Press

Acknowledgements

Copyright illustrations are reproduced by kind permission of the following:

F.W.O. Bauch Ltd. (36)
British Library, Reference Division (1, 15)
Trustees of the British Museum (2, 3)
Commonwealth Institute, London (5)
Basil Douglas Ltd. (28)
EMS (London) Ltd. (43)
Essex County Newspapers Ltd.; pupils of Essex schools (12, 18, 20, 21, 23, 26)
HHH Ltd.; Clive Barda; Susan Milan (9)
Embassy of the Indonesian Republic (29)
Ronald James (10)
Claude Delorme (30)
National Gallery, London (24)
National Museum of Denmark (4)
Paul Popper Ltd. (19)
Science Museum, London; Crown Copyright (35)
John Scott; Karen Dandy (22)
Dido Senger; the Kodaly Quartet (17)
Sky (31)
John Thomson; Decca Record Co. Ltd. (37, 38)
Victoria & Albert Museum; Crown Copyright (6, 13)
Yorkshire Post; John Jenner (27)

The remaining illustrations are the copyright of the author, who would like to thank the following for their co-operation:

Colchester Borough Council (14)
Students of the Dolmetsch Summer School (8, 16)
Judith Harris (11)
Valerie James (7)
Barbara Thompson & Dill Katz of "Paraphernalia" (33, 34)
Trygg Tryggvason; University of East Anglia (40, 41, 42)

Index